Poetry Even Your Mother Would Approve

(And other writings)

POETRY EVEN
YOUR MOTHER
WOULD APPROVE

Chaz Van Heyden

Contents

Contents

This Book of Poetry and Essays
is dedicated to Lynn Stewart
My sister

Forward

In Poetry My Mother Would've Approved and Poetry My Mother Would Not Have Approved the author wrote freely of his life, his perceptions about life and the sensations we all live for in Life.

PEYMWA continues the same way adding more of the sublime to the earthy poetry of its predecessors. Here however the view is towards more of what the greater number of souls can find real about life and lucidly stated in poetic terms. He's borrowed from the earlier works to round out this book of poetry, and I believe he has done an admirable job of blending.

Editor
Frank A. Carlyle

Preface

I chose to dedicate this volume of poetry to my sister, but in all fairness to all poetry lovers because you deserve good poetry.

It is my fondest belief that any individual can be poetic. Some of us choose not to reveal this ability to others, whereas some of us gladly take delight in exposing our poetic thoughts to others. The latter I recommend as excellent ongoing positive therapy that can offset life's vagaries and vicissitudes.

But don't cease exposing your poetic side, your poetic inclinations after first attempts. No, no, no. Just keep on being poetic. That's the only way I know of conquering any reticence one may have to inform others of your poetic preferences. Many more will be glad you did, than those who might titter and whisper. So, be brave and just say it. Get it out, and live longer and happier for it.

Poetry Even Your Mother Would Approve

(And other writings)

Spring

I Love Spring

When I think of

Birth and Semen and

New born infants and

Joyous pleasure from

Union of Man and Woman

I Love Spring

When the air

Turns alive

Radiating that certain

'Something' which

Tells of a stirring, a

New beginning.

And Bright is the future

As bright are The days.

I Love Spring.

It's the time

For Fraternity and

Worldly calm.

As the pollen

Floats to its

Best destiny by air

I am born by The Spirits to

My next creation -

To my subsequent

Intriguing affair.

The Audition

Actor: "I flush three times a day."

Director: "Cut, CUT! It's I *brush* three times a day. Take three!"

Actor: "I blush three times a day."

Director: For the love of Hubbard!!! It's *brush*, not blush.
Do IT again!

Actor: "I thrust three times a day."

Director: "&%*#@&*"

Dirt After Awhile

A person who won't even
flirt once Is a trial.

They'll never kick up their
Heels in Style.

Probably wind up with nothing
But dirt after awhile.

Go With The Flow

'A' stream of consciousness is
A misnomer. Life is THE
Stream of Consciousness, falling
Pitching, running, babbling,
Gurgling over and around rocks,
Branches, dug outs. Coursing,
Always coursing to the next
Destination.

Lie Down For Awhile

I'm going to lie down for awhile then
I'm going to smile for awhile, then
I'm going to rise for awhile and
Surprise for a while, even
Devise for awhile plus
Surmise for awhile.
Then I'm gonna trundle a bit
Bundle a bit and fondle a bit;
Masticate awhile,
Assimilate awhile, then I'm going to
Pollinate* for awhile and after,
Contemplate for awhile.
Then I'll cleanse and purify for awhile,
Nourish the body for awhile,
Exercise for awhile and
Lie down for awhile.

Following this activity, I'm
Going to reflect for awhile,
Remit for awhile and
Restore things for awhile. *Then*
I'm going to smile some more,
Contemplate some more, and
Renew my goals some more,
Take what I devised for awhile and
Make it known to many for awhile.

.

See that all is well for awhile, and
Tell people that all is well for awhile.

Finally, I am going to consummate
My day for awhile planning, the
Next day for awhile, and then
Lie down for awhile.

I Once Was

Once I felt the tainted saint, no more
Once I was bruised. I a'int, no more
Once was I a worn out 'plaint, no more
A tepid boy, used to faint, no more.

Once I possessed a delirious doctrine,
Once I lived by feast or famine.
And once I feared dying the gamin,
But now I can look and also examine.

I once was afraid to decide or commit,
Once I didn't know where I fit.
And once I could not even sit,
But now my days are sunny lit.

I Thought That I Needed

I thought that I needed to smile,
and laugh occasionally,
to be happy,

be nice to people,
take care of myself,
do good things,
go to school,
do my homework,
keep my nose clean.

I thought that if I bowed to dignitaries,
obeyed policemen,
respected my elders,
listened to authority,
saluted the flag,
voted regularly,
said thank you for gifts,
I could get along in Life,

I *also* thought that if I,
Kept my body clean,
Brushed my teeth regularly,
Got check ups every six months,
didn't drink much,
ate moderately,
exercised daily,
spoke *conservatively*,
I could live long, that I would be all right,
and I could be Happy.

I thought that if I
Kept my body clean,
Brushed my teeth regularly,
Got check ups every six months,
didn't drink much,
ate moderately,
exercised daily,
spoke *conservatively*,
I could live long, that I would be all right,
and I could be Happy.

I thought that if I saved money
invested wisely,
minded my own business,
read good books,
minimized TV
avoided bars,
visited museums and galleries,
    occasionally...
I could maintain a measure of success.

I also thought that,
To know God
I must not sin,
I must be charitable,
I should attend church,
Help the poor,
Be a good person,
Not start fights and pray,
Then I would be all right, and
I could be Happy.

What I _finally_ discovered is:

 ALL I needed... was TO BE!

BETTER MAN

Do you like the social graces?

Can you read behind the faces

When you meet the effacing ones

And the disgraced ones among

The smiling faces?

Then you're a better man.

Do you tend toward politeness?

Then you might wend between

The social shyness and

Sidestep the skeptical dryness...

Of the social graces, and be a

Better man.

Are you a sympathetic distruster of

Those who strut and bluster?

Can you be noble to the ignoble,

And listen to a tirade

Without turning a different shade?

Then you're a better man.

Not Necessarily a Dream

And somewhere a man is

Holding your beautiful face,

His hands so gently padding

Its cheeks with

Soft...and –

There, and there and

Everywhere with

Soft Kisses and

Putting his lips to

Your lips one

Molecule at a time

And it takes forever

These moments to

Arrive – it takes forever

And I wait and we wait,

But it takes forever

These moments to arrive.

How Long Is A Second?

The time it takes to flip a light switch.

The time it takes to snap fingers twice.

Drop a penny on a table from ten inches.

Say "Thank You".

Say "Goodbye".

Say "I had a nice time".

One half to one third the time most TV's turn on,

And the time it takes to turn it off.

The time it takes to knock on a closed door before entering.

The time it takes to smile at a stranger who is look-ing at you.

Does The World Need Pulp Fiction?

Does The World Need Pulp Fiction
I asked as I read.
Not if you're illiterate
Or just plain dead.

But what if you're sitting
Alone in your room
Starving for Adventure
To escape the gloom?

A dangerous voyage
Through piratical waters
A dash and tumble to
Save ransomed daughters.

A dizzying drop
From 10,000 feet
To a platform on earth
The size of a seat.

The chute won't open
And cold are your feet.
You hold your breath
To see what fate metes.

I close the book
Still blinking with awe
At the pulp fiction characters
Who seldom draw the long bowe.

I go back to my
Cubicle and the office friction
And think no more
Does the world need pulp fiction?

The Myth of Evil and Darkness

Darkness is not bad.
It is that way by association.
Darkness is very good! Especially to
A pair of lovers wrapped in a cozy beach
Blanket on a balmy stretch of sand by
The sea under a twinkling nite sky.

No, darkness is that which existed before
Light came along, which was when you were
Still thinking about what a Sun or Meteor
Might do to the spacescape, for space is
Not lit after it is made other than by suns or
Cosmic explosions.

And forget not how many beautiful
Photographs would never be seen by
Human eyes 'ere there was no darkness
To let the negative and print be developed.
Think! No National Geographic or Playboy or
Car and Driver unless darkness was Good.

And lastly and most deeply, how can one
Avoid the truth of darkness in the womb?
Our very fountainhead of existence!
Dreary yes, but not evil by itself.

Not a test tube with all the incandescent
Beauty abounding could take the place of
The mother's womb.

So give darkness its due.
It's no Fu Manchu.
What would light be without its milieu?

98% VEGETARIAN

Have you seen,

Have you heard?

The advent of

Pig's knuckles is the word.

Pig's knuckles are Coming again!

As I picked up a pair

The Asian man confidently

Stared, behind the steam

Fogged barriere.I sat down, and found

They're fatty, they're meaty

And tasty. Not what I feared.

Of course this took place

Long ago. I'm a vegetarian now,

I won't eat pig or cow.

Well almost so...

Pig? Oh NO!

Pig's knuckles?

Let's go!

Sometimes

I get tears easily (for practically no reason at all; and then again) for the heart-break stories, such as this famous one:

An editor once challenged authors to write a six word story. Ernest Hemingway did and this is what he wrote:

Baby shoes, for sale, never used.

Do you get tears when you hear or read a story about the overcoming of human suffering? Or the overcoming of inadequate education? Those are the kind of tears I like to shed.

And even the simple act of seeing someone get what they have long dreamed for?

Have you ever experienced the joy of relief and new found energy when after a bout with flue or a long convalescence has ended?

What of a time when you mastered a skill that even you were on tenterhooks about?

I'm sure that you'll agree, if you can recollect any of these, that they are truly among the great reasons life is worth living.

Strategy

Recently I put my emotions in a jar
And left the lid slightly open.
So those who want to see and know
More about me can do so with ease,
While I can prevent any complete
Disclosure with only a superficial
Movement of my hand.

SUPERBOWLS

Openings
In the line are
Not just "openings"
They're super holes.

AND lest we forget
Everything at
The SUPERBOWL
Is likewise
Superior:

Cheerleaders are
Super-girls
The players are
Super-men,

(Hot) Dogs are
Super-hot
And beverages
Super-cold.

Cheers are
Super-CHEERS
And beers
SUPER beers.

If played in
Florida
The mascots are
Komodo Dragons,

Which we know are
SUPER-LIZARDS.

Touchdowns known
As a T-D
Are reported
As S-TDs!

And so it goes
For Everything is SUPER
At SUPERBOWLS.

What Chance The Fall Leaf

Pulled down to earth by gravity,
Soaked and weighed down by rains.
Blown down by gusts mightily.
What chance for a leaf remains?

Like a leaf are we?

When chill wind of misfortune
Blows mysterious
Upon our saddened face,
When mildest of error can
Condemn us to disgrace.
And obligation's weight
Bears semblance to
A Mountain of slate,
What chance have we?

Out of the dark and
Nebulous dreams that
Come to haunt us,
From twists of fate
Calamities insult us,

When regret itself
Is no longer salve
For life's injuries
That pierce us,

What then are we?
The Fall leaf?
Who are we—
Who are we indeed!

What are we,
Regarded so anonymously—
Handled so ignominiously.
That we should be treated
So indifferently?

None but the wisest,
The strongest, the best,
Suited to oppose the
Arrows & Strings of
Outrageousness.

None but the most
Cunning and none but
The most deserving.

The leaf, like any other
Life has its *chances* and
We have our *chances.*

Wind Chimes

Can you hear that-

Can you hear that tinkling?

The tintinnabulating treasure of Sound.

Wind chimes.

When I think about them I feel good.

The wind blows,

The chimes *speak* to me.

I'm quieted.

Back down the centuries to a Village,

In Asia I'm reminded of another time, and

Another place,

When the wind blew

Across a mountain top overlooking a verdant

Valley bustling with happy people.

Marriage Proposal

Don't want to be
Married for eternity.
I care not to be
Married 'til death
Do us part.

I'd rather be married
To you for the purpose of
Enjoying your love.

Until the purpose becomes
Completely Tart.

CHARLIES WORLD

If the world I could brazenly face
And smooth by a little its fitful pace
Then Justice would I do
For myself and men
To put happiness and more
Laughter within their ken.

If all the world is a stage
Then let the plays never end
And let Charlie's world append,
To ours, to yours, to theirs.

When we turn the corner
Let's do that skid, let's
Lift that leg—shake it kid.
And twitch our upper lip
Mustache or not.
Wink often and hard
Our fedoras tip.

If I should the world brazenly face
It shall be Charlie's World,
And my world
And nothing ever again
Like the commonplace.

The Noose

The news has brought
Me to grief again.

I'm apathetic about
Life today like
Yesterday.
Oh why do I
Need the news?

The First Page
Is the 1st stage
That like a booster
Sends me down
The tubes faster.

If I were a reporter
Or a cocaine snorter,
I'd enjoy telling
Everyone the news

But since I eschew
Making people into glue,
I'll refrain from
Pouring out the soo'.

A man once said
You can practically
Raise the dead
By restraining daily
Papers and the ed.

So it came
To pass, and it
Happened very fast,
Ridding the black and
White became a
Sensation overnight
The community rising
Above the black
Clouds grasp.

So to all who have
Paid your dues,
I hope this ditty,
About a thing clearly
Shitty, will prompt you
To take your vitamins
But not the news.

My View

In my view I know what
I must do.

Things all of them
Which normally I
Eschew.

The lifelong
Contemporary residue.

It will take
Years and
Probably a clever
Tune or two.

But, in my mind
I know what
I must do.

Other Writings

You Can Have Your Cake and Eat It

I moved recently and found that I no longer had a "grinder" with which to pulverize my grains freshly before cooking my porridge in the morning.

So, I thought about how I could get them ground without having to go out and buy another coffee grinder, which is what I really normally use.

K____r has as do many grocery stores a coffee grinder. And this is how a new recipe came about for morning hot porridge. In order to use the store coffee grinder some of the coffee bits will get into the grain flour. *This* is obvious.

However this is perfect because some mornings I like a cup of hot coffee -- mostly for the flavor.

So I didn't clean out the Kroger grinder first but just poured in my grains and... Voila! Coffee flavored porridge.

It looks better darker too.

Of course I bought a small amount of French Roast in exchange for using their grinding facility and it served to "clean out" the grain dust left that would ordinarily surprise the next customer who expected only powered coffee to come out of the grinder.

To coin a new phrase: "You can have your cake and eat it and even like it."

The Legend of Adonis and Venus

There once was a powerful being with unlimited abilities. This being decided that there should be a perfect embodiment of his beingness and so he created Adonis and Venus, since without something to compare to he would not for sure know that Adonis was perfect. Then when Adonis met Venus this powerful being made Adonis love Venus and Venus fell in love with Adonis.

They procreated and the result was Vedonis a perfect duplicate of Adonis, and Avenus a perfect duplicate of Venus so they would always have the pairing to admire. They lived happily ever after, UNTIL another powerful being thought to rearrange things, since that being's creations were not being so much admired. He created Thalidomide and permeated an apple with it. Then with powerful intention got Venus to partake of the apple, even though her creator had with his unlimited abilities foreknown the intention of his adversary and warned Venus not to eat any apples.

Thus came about the horrible unimaginable. The next creation of Adonis and Venus was a FREAK! Not understanding the cause of this mishap they chose to hide this mishap by giving it a name. MAN.

The Downside of Riches

I just got my new BMW outfitted with a theft proof alarm.

Fittingly I'm in one of the parking tiers at the _____ Super Mall and a earthquake hits.

Naturally...because the lot is "quakeproof" I survive death only to have my ears blasted away by thousands of alarms going off simultaneously.

Just then a fellow in a black jacket drives by in my BMW grinning!

The Age of Enlightenment began in 1969. It's taken four decades for anything approximating it in politics, or should I say Political Science (a true subject). Don't muff it now. Vote, not for who will *most likely win*, vote for the candidate--nominate the candidate that by their record alone, follows the U.S. Constitution more, and more consistently than any one else running. Read many books and blogs, and be educated about the constitution. (Read that again a few times also.) Let no one or no thing prevent you from total understanding of the game.

I Do, I Don't Understand

I'm shaving today and I notice the setting for the shaving blades hasn't changed in 37 years...well not exactly, since the manufacturer didn't make an electric razor with adjustable blade depth 37 years ago.

One day long time ago I tried adjusting those blades to see which setting was the best. There's nine of them. That's right, nine different separate settings.

The only one that worked for me was #9, the deepest setting -the one with the most blade showing, similar thing to a table saw except that facial hair is pretty easy to cut once it gets above the surface of the skin.

So, I'm thinking what are those other eight settings doing there – who's running around with a (1) or (2) setting, must be pretty effeminate because my whiskers aren't all that stiff compared to some guys I know!

It's not the same with a lawn mower 'cause there you want some of the grass left above the ground and the settings give you a choice how much.

And that concept definitely wouldn't work for the ladies. They want it all gone. In fact, you'd be so much happier if it didn't grow at all.

There's nothing more useless to a woman than hair on her knee caps, unless it's a man who uses a # 1 setting on his shaver.

No Headlights

Ever try driving a car at night with the headlamps turned off? Like walking down the sidewalk blind-folded only a lot scarier.

Well, it can be done...by the light of a full moon as once occurred to me one night coming down from a 11,000 foot altitude road out of Denver. I decided I would drive all night through the night non-stop until I reached LA and then complete the journey the next morning. What began as an experiment turned into one of the most pleasurable and memorable experiences of my life.

Everyone loves driving cars, right? Well, yes of course provided we understand that there are no absolutes. The odd, shocking and most beautiful aspect of all is the fact that without the car head-lamps on, the road ahead in full moonlight is visible for miles all illuminated to the same degree. You see, the back glare of the headlamps obscures the road further out than the beam, so turning off the headlamps suddenly and completely immerses one in a surreal world but having no hidden dangers whatsoever!

Warm was the night and warm seemed the moonlight. The two-seater Suzuki hummed along with no passenger yap yap to intrude upon the immensely satisfying quiet, enhanced by the softness of wind flowing outside and around the car. If ever there were a moment of *oneness* with nature this was that moment.

The Power of Chicken Soup

I remember very distinctly, one day, when I was not feeling well...I was down. I decided to make my own chicken soup from scratch. Included a whole host of vegetables in it.

Got out the pots, the cutting devices. No recipe. Just *Hell Bent For Leather*. Started with some poultry. Put that on the stove and boiled for about two hours. Took the broth and pieces of chicken, which fell apart from the bone, and set that aside. Then I added vegetables. Tons of vegetables. Bok choy, spinach with the stems trimmed. Celery diced up, zucchini diced up. Just everything you could imagine. Cilantro. I had about 17 different vegetables in there. I poured that combination into the home made chicken broth. Simmered that for about fifteen minutes. Wala! Talk about a *resurrection*. My demeanor was not the same and remained positive for a long time, in fact indefinitely afterwards.

If I had a hundred million gallons of that soup, I could SAVE the world. Save the planet and make a change in a lot of peoples' lives.

Let's see...did I include onions?

Annie Oakley Rides Again

Last year I was contemplating some rather startling discoveries about myself. Usually this doesn't happen but once or twice in a lifetime for most of us. But this was so startling and so unique that I mention it here to edify those of you who read this.

For as long as I can remember, I thought that other people were in the know about most things, for example: how to make a great catered dinner, how to make a stereo from scratch, how to paint, how to compose music and songs, how to write good fiction, even how to build a house.

Then last year, not long ago really, it came to me in a flash, literally a flash. I can do most of these things better than the people I thought knew how to do them.

Not a brag essentially, since I acknowledged it to myself alone. "Anything you can do I can do better" is a bit of a boast, but if one CAN do it better what's the sense of saying, "well...er...I guess I can do it better than you"

Preamble

I have a preamble I recite to the driver when I get on public transit. It goes: "I am depositing this money and taking a seat on this bus, but at the same time I am entrusting my life to you to get me safely to my destination." This usually gets a nod or sometimes a surprised look. If it doesn't and the driver looks a bit pale or is staring at me and says nothing, I turn around and get off that bus. And find a better one.

Are Conclusions Important?

Yes, otherwise this world would not exist.

Some people reach conclusions rather swiftly while others take a l-o-n-g time.

Two men are standing under a passing jet not looking above. The first man by the jet engine sound alone has already concluded that

it is a jet airplane
it is a military jet
probably a fighter
not from a nearby floating aircraft carrier
and about 2000 feet above,
its general compass direction that it is headed.

The other man has yet to decide if it is in fact a jet plane.

No conscious action, no effort is put forth by humans before a calculation and a conclusion of the effort involved. That's how important conclusions are.

Compulsory Education—A Failure

It has been observed that anything which is done automatically is better done by hand. So it is and has been and with worsening results with education when done compulsorily. The guilds of the 12th through the 18th century were exceedingly successful in educating its apprentice students in skills necessary to carry on survival in a maturing society, raising its head from the Dark Ages.

Where we went wrong was, not in providing school houses for our children in which they could read books and ask questions of a preceptor but, in passing laws making it compulsory to attend. In fact our civilization began, almost imperceptibly, to decline the moment we as adults agreed to *be forced to* sending our children to school legally, and of course accepting fiscal funding through taxation for this encroachment on the rights of children and parents.

"Life is the best educator", is a saying that over and over again has been accepted by the multitudes, and this is not true in any sense. Life does not induce anyone to think better, act better, respond faster, create more: only the individual's will to conquer his environment, only the individual's determination to achieve completely that which the individual most wants to achieve is the chief inducement to think better, act better, respond faster, create more. What life does teach is what happens if one does not "get along with others." And this lesson has the appearance of being wise, when in fact it has the opposite effect. Examine the lives of any man or woman who has established themselves equitably in life, who are productive members of society; typical men and women as well as great men and women who are self-reliant, self-generated persons, and in that examination will be still found 1) the willingness to learn from their own observation and 2) competence derived from applying their willingness to observe.

When any honest research is done, the only time compulsory education worked, worked when it was used solely for military or religious purposes. Today and for the future these uses are superfluous necessities as a compulsory practice. If a person can't be trusted to align him or herself with an abiding philosophy about life then that person isn't long for this world and is a detriment to the society.

For the most part compulsory education is regimentation as it was in its inception. Men need to think freely, act freely and perceive that they are free to do so even in a society which has given in to compulsory practices such as compulsory education. We did away with conscription, finally, and likewise we would be well advised to do away with compulsory education, even compulsory health care.

What to do in their absence? That requires diligent research and testing. Which requires, naturally the self-determined, non-compulsory desire to discover and learn. Whose is *not* willing to do this?

Is It Natural

Is it natural for a person to want to communicate aesthetically?

The answer would be in two parts:

1) Is it natural for a person to communicate?

To that I would give an emphatic YES.

2) What does it mean to communicate aesthetically?

Well what does aesthetics mean is next: In an aesthetic manner, Therefore we have

Aesthetic – Def. A The beautiful qualities of something (for now we'll leave out the academic definitions of "principles on which an artist's work is based".)

And what may we ask is beautiful?   Great and necessary question.

Well, for a saltwater fisherman, the prospects of living in the middle of a desert would not be beautiful since it not only deprives him of his livelihood (and passion) but it also deprives him of making use of a boat and wind and seafaring conditions as a game he likes playing.

So, it is not enough to rely just on the old adage, "Beauty is in the eye of the beholder" since some people are blind and some don't perceive the world

Beauty to be "beauty" must compliment the perceiver of it in some way. It certainly must bring added pleasure without which life is not as pleasurable or interesting.

A rodeo guy would probably shirk listening to such a sonnet. He would not find any beauty in it.

When we go out on a "date" or to an "affair" we most often want to dress properly, give a good appearance to others, and again be perceived as not being at odds with the environment. Dressing for public viewing, our appearance is after all a communication.

Then we have those who use various avenues of expression, such as music and movies and book writing to further their message or emotions about particular subjects in a way that we might very well find objectionable. However, if there are like minded persons receiving the communication via these media then the maxim yet holds true.
Violently worded rap music, for example, appeals to a segment of our society. And it uses song and musical composition with its rhythm and dynamics just as a symphony by Bela Bartok or Tchaikovsky would. No doubt the originators want to communicate along the lines that are going to be pleasing to buyers of their music. And to some degree they succeed.

So, in this short essay, I have proposed a question, which may not have *ever* been proposed publicly, and answered it.

Aesthetics Is Where MAN Ultimately Finds His Salvation

It may turn out eventually that aesthetics is where Man ultimately finds his salvation. And it would be fitting if he did, for certainly it has been through the misuse of aesthetics that he has floundered and foundered. Examine for instance how the invention of the guillotine was so widely and wildly received because it was clean swift and thorough in its lethal use. An aesthetic but with what as its product. Sudden death. The Nobel Peace Prize created by Alfred Nobel, a chemist, invented dynamite. It is used constructively and *destructively* by terrorists and assassins. I'm quite sure both uses are seen as *beautiful* when it carries out the intention behind it. And, isn't a huge brilliant mushroom of atomic gases and radiation seen as startlingly lovely to anyone who is many miles away. Do you think perhaps one consideration remains that many scientists loved the idea of "the bomb" and still do?

How can Man use aesthetics to send him toward a more desirable existence? For one, several hospitals have for some time arranged the playing of soothing music inside maternity wards, where the babies are discovered to be less colic, less temperamental. They rest longer and better. This has now evolved into the additional discovery that it works for most patients in hospital type atmospheres. What person doesn't feel more tranquil, even more alive in front of and viewing a fine painter's masterpiece. I get that way seeing that quality of art reproduced in a digital form as well. We're noticing an upswing in LIVE television programming where dancing and vocalizing is praised copiously and the artists get better and better as the shows continue. We should never pass up the occasion to complement a quality product or service. That is the aesthetic we want to encourage.

Lastly there is *beauty* to self mastery. Poets and philosophers have written and spoken of it a myriad number of times. It is possibly a goal which if a larger proportion of our society made it there duty to accomplish, concurrently, we would see a swift rise in the culture's stability.

By The Time I Leave This World

BY THE TIME I leave this world, even at a great age, I expect that I will be as healthy as when I entered it: not senile, not an invalid, not feeble minded, not in pain, ill or disfigured. And not sexually impotent. This is no doubt at variance with the bulk of humanity if the bulk of humanity even considers the subject.

Shockingly, I surmise for most, I have had this expectancy since infancy, possibly much longer. Although I can not with complete certainty state that this has always been the case, I can say that a version of this statement has always been a part of my character.

Truly, I have never seen a reason for gradual decline of the human condition into toothless, blind, tasteless and helpless dependency, as Shakespeare so adequately describes at the end of his eloquent soliloquy beginning with these words, "All the world is a stage, and all the men and women merely players etc."

In fact, much like the character of Benjamin Button, I anticipate the gradual reverse of the above cycle at the end of life, completely doing away with tombstones and graveyards, sextons and funeral parlors. Won't that be a boon? It makes for a much cleaner, even perfect resolution. Instead of the progeny looking on with dismay as their parents wilt and wrinkle, become childlike and incontinent, they will probably see them disappear as healthy embryos. Who knows perhaps a beloved ritual of eating the embryos will emerge and be the standard instead of burial in a molding coffin or incineration and dumping into watery graves.

Personally I expect to have a bushy head of hair again and get back to wearing leather jackets while riding motorcycles as I did quite a lot in my late thirties and early forties. And just today I was stopped into a clothing store to use their rest room and I spied a beautiful women's leather jacket and coming out of the RR I asked a sales clerk if the store had any leather jackets for men. We walked over to a rack and the first one she picked looked great and fit perfectly. You wouldn't ever guess the sale price. One third the way there. Hah!

The Face of God

No man has seen the face of God. This we have heard many times. But. if we change the word "the" to the letter "a" we can state:

Man has seen a face of God.

In fact, Man has seen and does see billions of faces of God.

We are all children of God. That's very familiar too. Also we know that children eventually grow up. Therefore *mature* children of God will ultimately be ?

As yee consider so shall yee be.

POETRY MY MOTHER WOULD'VE APPROVED

C. VAN HEYDEN

Pick up your copy of the companion book of poetry, and get
ready for the next in series:
POETRY MY MOTHER WOULD NOT HAVE APPROVED

Now Available at Amazon.com

www.ingramcontent.com/pod-product-compliance
Lightning Source LLC
Chambersburg PA
CBHW070536130626
46555CB00003B/1444